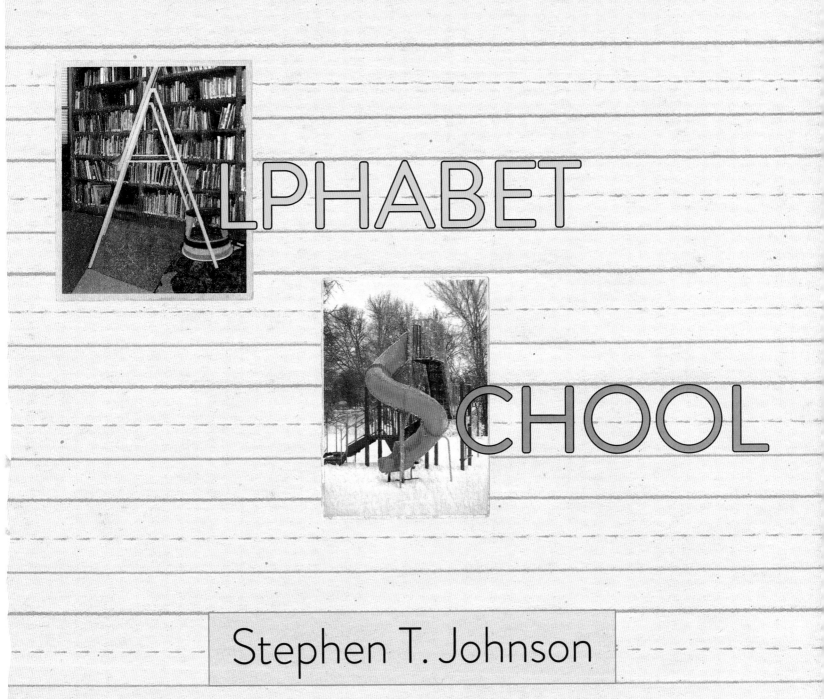

Alphabet School

Stephen T. Johnson

A Paula Wiseman Book

SIMON & SCHUSTER BOOKS FOR YOUNG READERS

New York London Toronto Sydney New Delhi

To Paula Wiseman and Laurent Linn, for their constant belief, support, and patience during the lengthy journey of creating this book, and to all my wonderful teachers who over the years taught, guided, and enlightened with grace, intelligence, and humor, and helped send me forth into the world

SIMON & SCHUSTER BOOKS FOR YOUNG READERS
An imprint of Simon & Schuster Children's Publishing Division
1230 Avenue of the Americas, New York, New York 10020
Copyright © 2015 by Stephen T. Johnson
All rights reserved, including the right of reproduction in whole or in part in any form.
SIMON & SCHUSTER BOOKS FOR YOUNG READERS is a trademark of Simon & Schuster, Inc.
For information about special discounts for bulk purchases,
please contact Simon & Schuster Special Sales at 1-866-506-1949 or business@simonandschuster.com.
The Simon & Schuster Speakers Bureau can bring authors to your live event.
For more information or to book an event, contact the Simon & Schuster Speakers Bureau
at 1-866-248-3049 or visit our website at www.simonspeakers.com.
Book design by Laurent Linn
The text for this book is set in Brandon Grotesque.
The illustrations for this book were created with monoprints on paper and digitally enhanced.
Manufactured in China
0615 SCP
10 9 8 7 6 5 4 3 2 1
Library of Congress Cataloging-in-Publication Data
Johnson, Stephen, 1964-
Alphabet school / Stephen T. Johnson.
pages cm
Summary: Explore the alphabet in everyday objects found at school in this dazzling picture book. A classroom companion to celebrated artist Stephen Johnson's Caldecott Honor book *Alphabet City*, this alphabet book is a tour de force in the genre. There is much more to this book than meets the eye!
ISBN 978-1-4169-2521-7 (hardcover)
1. Alphabet books—Juvenile literature. I. Title.
PE1155.J647 2015
421'.1—dc23
2014041731

first
edition

AUTHOR'S NOTE

The alphabet, with its twenty-six letters reordered, forms written words and phrases that can open up ideas in our minds. The letters of the alphabet are also visual forms. When we discover them in different contexts, the connections we draw from our experiences allow us to see the world anew.

Creative connections to letters may arise in subtle and unintended ways. A comet—the logo design for a school gymnasium—that enters a central circle painted on a wooden floor might look a lot like the letter Q. In the same way, an ordinary asphalt playground covered with infinitely shifting wood chips over hopscotch delineations might momentarily reveal the letter *D*. These fortuitous discoveries and subsequent explorations into their implications open our eyes to the world. This is how *Alphabet City* and *Alphabet School* came to be.

Since the publication of my book *Alphabet City* in 1995, I have been delighted by the creative booklets, imaginative drawings, alliterative letters, and intuitive photographs sent to me by students, teachers, librarians, and parents who have used the images I generated to draw associations with their own worlds and in particular to their schools. Inspired by these and my continuous exploration of places, forms, and ideas, I returned to schools for their visual potential and collective memories in the past, now, and in the future.

Then one day, my daughter brought home from school her lunch bag with partially eaten bits of vegetables and fruit and a half-eaten peanut butter and jelly sandwich, the very one I had made earlier that morning, which formed a perfect letter G! I knew then I had to make this book.

I hope that my images will inspire children and adults to look at their surroundings in a fresh and playful way. In doing so they will discover for themselves juxtapositions of scale, harmonies of shadows, rhythms, colorful patterns in surface textures, and joy in the most mundane and unexpected places by transcending the day-to-day and unearthing life's hidden beauty.

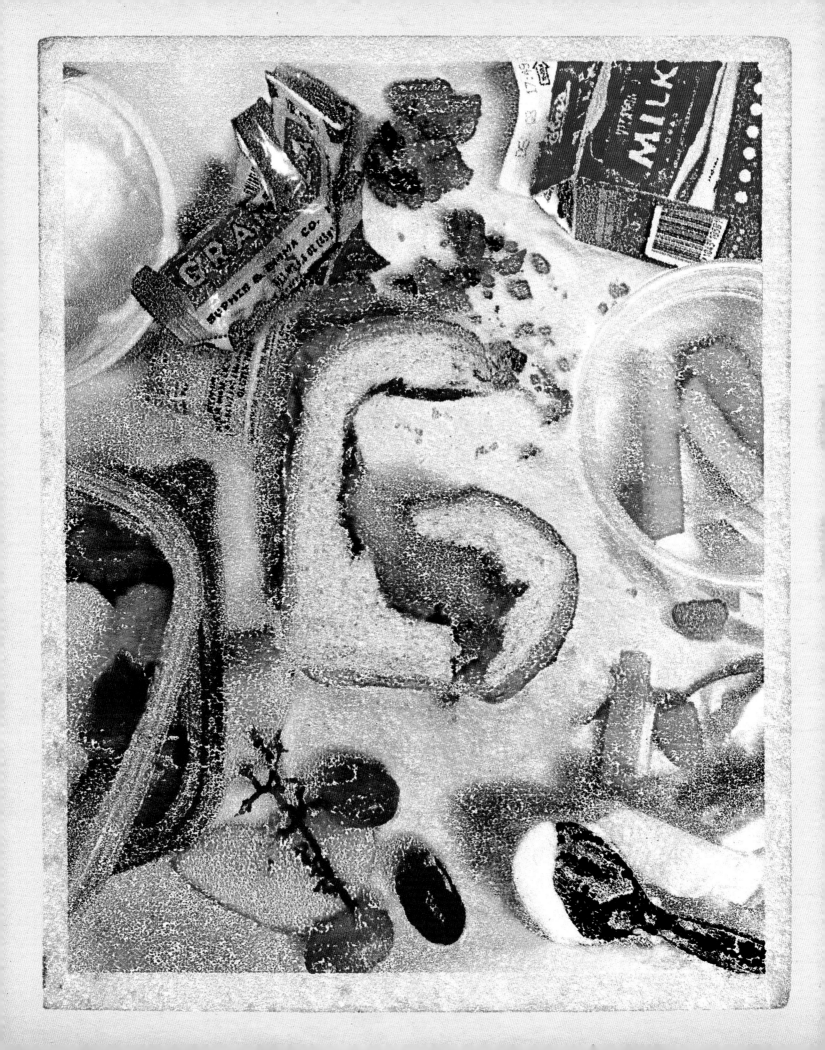

Bb Cc Dd Ee

Jj Kk Ll M

Qq Rr Ss Uu

Xx Yy Zz 34567

Chart

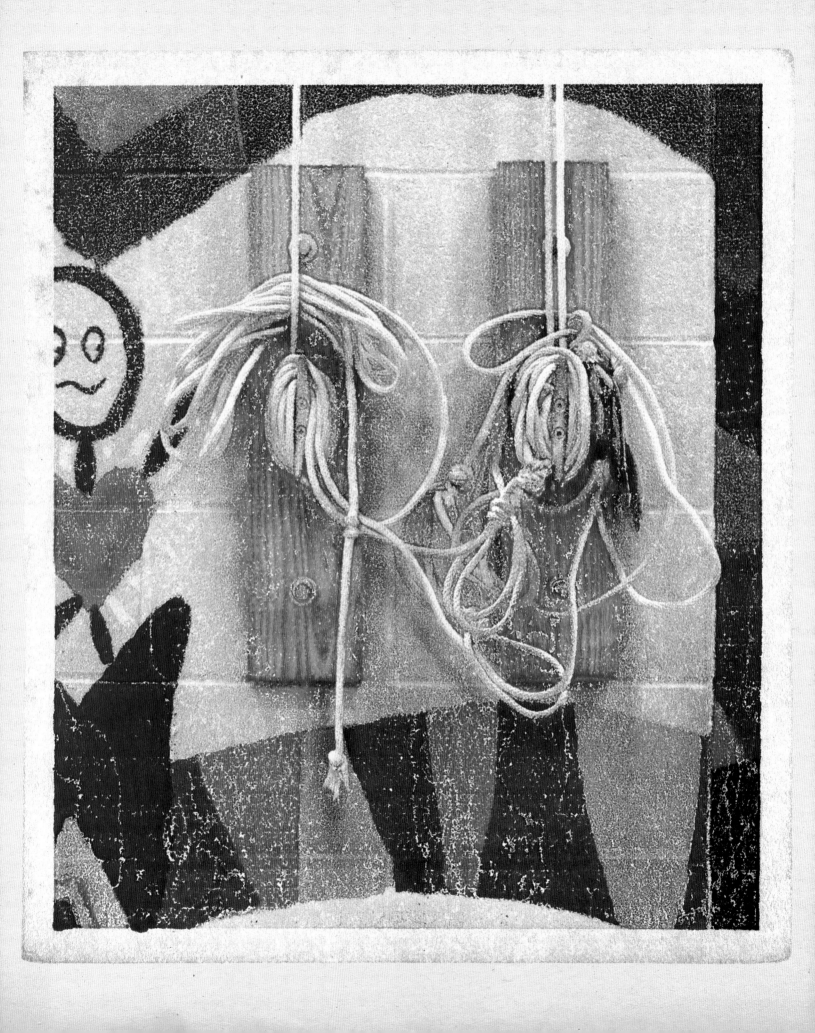